HAPPY CHRISTMAS POYRY

POYraz

This book belongs to

Poyraz

About Katha

Katha, a nonprofit organization working with and in story and storytelling since 1988, is one of India's top publishing houses. Katha's main focus is on introducing an array of writings from the many oral and written traditions of India to children, ages 0-17. Classy productions, child-friendly layouts and superb illustrations go in tandem with excellent writing. Katha works with 6,000 Friends of Katha and a growing pool of writers, translators and literary enthusiasts. Our constant striving is for greater reach and impact amongst teachers and students, policy makers and the corporate sector.

Our mission: To enhance the joys of reading. To help every child realize his/her potential through community enriching, quality learning so that no child lives in poverty. To help break down gender, social, cultural and economic stereotypes through story and storytelling. And to enhance the role of translation as a counter-divisive tool in nation building.

Our belief: Stories help create friendships of a rare kind to culturelink people, faiths and creative impulses. Stories are the life-savers of future nations.

Our credo: Uncommon creativities for a common good.

to each her own

Vijaydan Detha

Art by Anita Hashemi Moghaddam

Translated from the Rajasthani
by Christi A Merrill, with Kailash Kabir

KATHA

Once upon a time and place there was a fresh water lake. And at the edge of this lake was a fisherman's hut.

The air was thick with the smell of fish. But the fisherman and his wife loved the smell.

Every day, the fisherwoman would fill her basket with fish and walk to the nearest town to sell them.

One day, as she was leaving, her husband said, "It looks like it will rain heavily. Hurry back. I fear the river will flood."

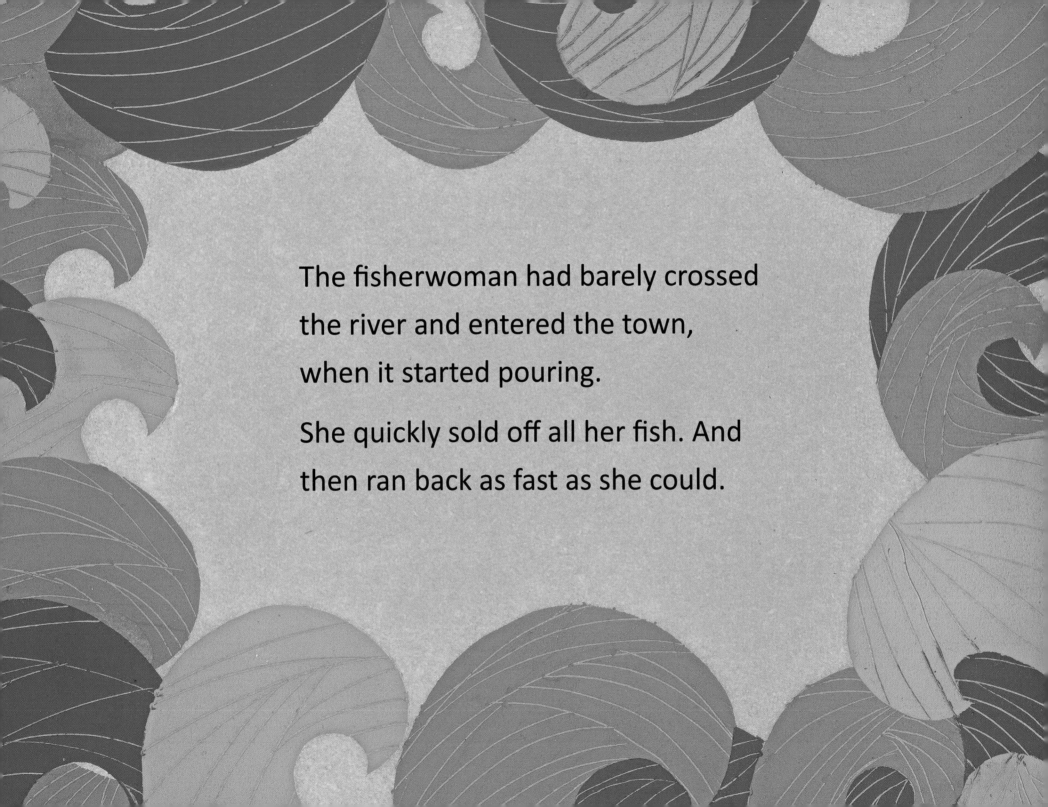

The fisherwoman had barely crossed the river and entered the town, when it started pouring.

She quickly sold off all her fish. And then ran back as fast as she could.

But the river already had big, big waves.

She turned away sadly. She could not go home now.

But where would she stay the night?

Just then the fisherwoman saw the gardener.

The gardener looked after the Raja's beautiful gardens.

She saw the fisherwoman's sad face and said, "The river has come up, no? But don't worry. Please come home with me."

The fisherwoman was happy and grateful.

As they walked, the gardener said, "You are so wet. You must be very cold."

The fisherwoman laughed, "We are like fish ourselves. No matter how wet, we are never cold!"

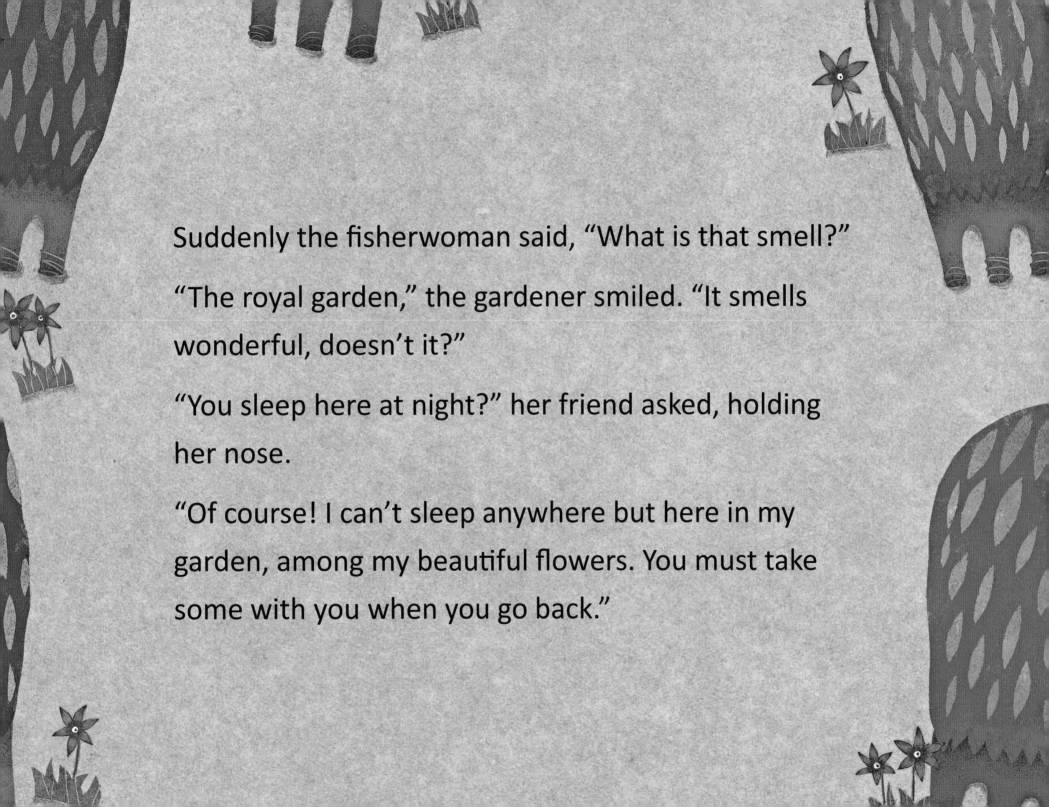

Suddenly the fisherwoman said, "What is that smell?"

"The royal garden," the gardener smiled. "It smells wonderful, doesn't it?"

"You sleep here at night?" her friend asked, holding her nose.

"Of course! I can't sleep anywhere but here in my garden, among my beautiful flowers. You must take some with you when you go back."

The fisherwoman was struggling to breathe as little as possible as she softly said, "You are very kind. But what would I do with flowers?"

"Why, you don't know how wonderful my flowers are! Touch one, and your fingertips will smell sweet for three days!" the gardener said.

Then she took her into a room next to the garden and said, "You sit here. I'll go and get you some dry clothes."

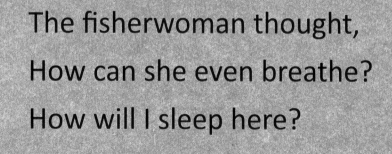

The fisherwoman thought,
How can she even breathe?
How will I sleep here?

Soon the gardener came back with some clean, dry clothes heaped with flowers.

The poor fisherwoman felt like vomiting.

Suddenly, the gardener sniffed the air sharply and wrinkled up her nose. "What's that awful smell?"

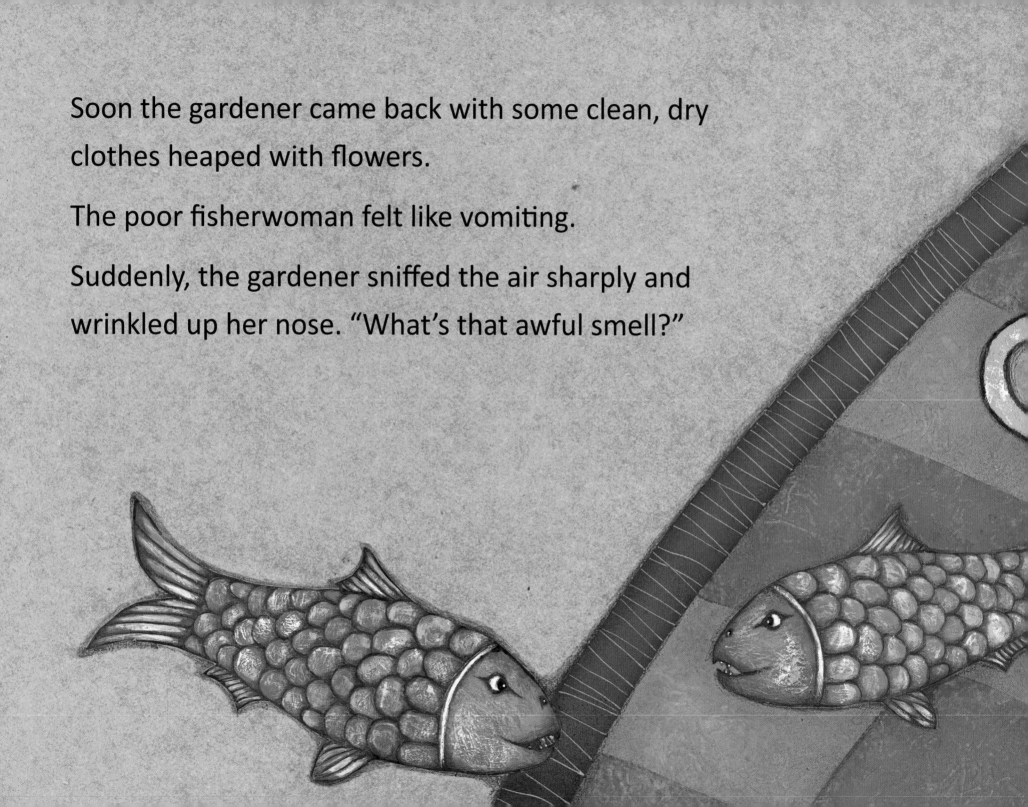

She looked around and saw the basket lying in the corner. "Why did you bring your empty basket inside?"

The gardener quickly took the basket outside the room.

What could the fisherwoman say?

They sat and ate their meal together.

How awful the gardener smelt, thought the fisherwoman.

The gardener too thought, How fishy that woman smells!

But of course both the women were too polite to say anything.

Meal over, the gardener took her
leave and went away to her room
with a big sigh of relief.

And away from the smell of fish,
she slept in her room on a bed of
sweet-smelling flowers.

The fisherwoman tossed and turned
and tried hard, but she could not sleep.

Then she quietly tip-toed outside
and brought her basket in. She
buried her nose into her fish basket.

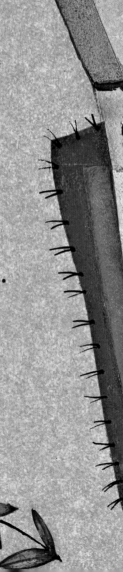

And soon she too was fast asleep!

Did you know?

This story is from India ...

7th largest country

1.2 billion people

Hindi and 28 other major languages

Women in sarees

Leading producer of milk and mangoes

Major producer of fish, tea and silk

Famous across the globe for its Kalbelia folk songs and dances

Curries, spices and sweets

Have you been to Taj Mahal, or visited the endless Thar desert yet?

These pictures are from Iran ...

18th largest country

79 million people

Persian and six other major languages

Leading producer of oil and pistachio

Finest producer and exporter of handmade carpets

Famous across the globe for the Radif of Persian music

Women in manteaus and headscarves

Kebabs, naan, tahdeeg cooked rice and sherbets

When you travel to Iran, don't forget to visit Persepolis and their famous Persian gardens.

In Hindi we say Namaste, and in English, Hello!

Do you know how people across India greet each other?

Match the greetings to their respective languages!

Marathi	Namaskara
Manipuri	Nomoshkar
Bengali	Kem Chho
Gujarati	Khurumjari
Tamil	Khamma Ghani Sa
Telugu	Salam Alaikum
Punjabi	Namaskar! Kasa Kay?
Rajasthani	Namaskaram
Urdu	Vanakkam
Kannada	Sat Sri Akal

Answers:
Marathi - Namaskar! Kasa Kay? | Manipuri - Khurumjari | Bengali – Nomoshkar
Gujarati - Kem Chho | Tamil – Vanakkam | Telugu - Namaskaram
Punjabi - Sat Sri Akal | Rajasthani - Khamma Ghani Sa
Urdu - Salam Alaikum | Kannada- Namaskara

Vijaydan Detha or Bijji as he is lovingly called, is a genius at recreating and retelling the stories he hears from fellow villagers of Borunda, near Jodhpur. He has written more than 800 short stories which have been translated into Hindi, English and other languages, including *Anokha Ped,* a collection of children's stories. 'To Each Her Own', written originally in Rajasthani as 'Aap Apri Sourabh,' is based on a story in *The Gospel of Ramakrishna*. Redolent of the desert sands, Detha's lively, wry and lyrical stories are rich in Rajasthani folklore, arts, music and dialects. He is the recipient of several awards including the Padmashri, the Sahitya Akademi Award and the Katha Chudamani Award.

Anita Hashemi Moghaddam is an acclaimed Iranian artist and painter who has illustrated for many magazines and publications. Her award-winning works have been exhibited internationally. She loves illustrating for children and taking part in art workshops.

Christi A Merrill is Assistant Professor, South Asian Literature at the University of Michigan. She translates from Hindi, Rajasthani, and French, and writes on translation too.

Kailash Kabir, a respected Hindi poet, has translated much of Vijaydan Detha's works into Hindi. He has also translated A K Ramanujan's *Folktales of India* from English to Hindi. He received the Sahitya Akademi National Award for Translation and the Rajasthan Sahitya Akademi Award for Poetry.

KATHA

First published in *Chouboli and Other Stories, Vol 2*, 2010
Copyright © Katha, 2012
Original story copyright © Vijaydan Detha, 2010
Illustrations copyright © Anita Hashemi Moghaddam, 2012
All rights reserved. No part of this book may be reproduced or utilized in any form without the prior written permission of the publisher.
Printed at Aegean Offset Printers, Noida (UP)
ISBN 978-81-89934-02-6

KATHA is a registered nonprofit devoted to enhancing the joys of reading amongst children and adults. Katha Schools are situated in the slums and streets of Delhi and tribal villages of Arunachal Pradesh.
A3 Sarvodaya Enclave, Sri Aurobindo Marg
New Delhi 110 017
Phone: 4141 6600 . 4182 9998 . 2652 1752
Fax: 2651 4373
E-mail: marketing@katha.org, Website: www.katha.org

Ten per cent of sales proceeds from this book will support the quality education of children studying in Katha Schools.
Katha regularly plants trees to replace the wood used in the making of its books.

Katha CHITrAKALA Award

Katha Chitrakala Awards recognize exemplary children's book illustrations and concepts. Artists with that magical eye and a way with colours, are invited to this international search for excellence – the only one of its kind in India – open to all image storytellers, emerging or established, to make an indelible mark in the world of children's books.

Today, Katha Chitrakala Awards boasts of an enthusiastic participation of over 300 illustrators from over 14 countries.

Katha has a real soft corner for kids. Which is why it ... create[s] such gorgeous picture books for children.

— Time Out

Katha Chitrakala Award 2009 for Outstanding Creativity

Geeta Dharmarajan | Art by Rajiv Eipe

DINOSAUR -LONG-AS -127-KIDS

Katha Chitrakala Award 2006 for Outstanding Creativity

The Famous Smile

Geeta Dharmarajan
Art by Rashin Kheiriyeh

Runner Up Katha Chitrakala Award 2009 for Outstanding Creativity

Diego Castellanos
Art by Paula Bossio

BALL Heaven

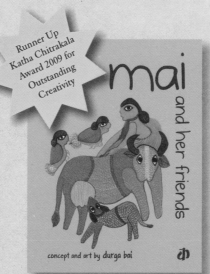

Runner Up Katha Chitrakala Award 2009 for Outstanding Creativity

mai and her friends

concept and art by durga bai

Runner Up Katha Chitrakala Award 2006 for Outstanding Creativity

RALEH AND THE SINGSONG CASTLE

Rizio Yohannan Raj | Art by Anahita Taymourian